dust bunny wants a friend

amy hevron

schwartz & wade books · new york

bye

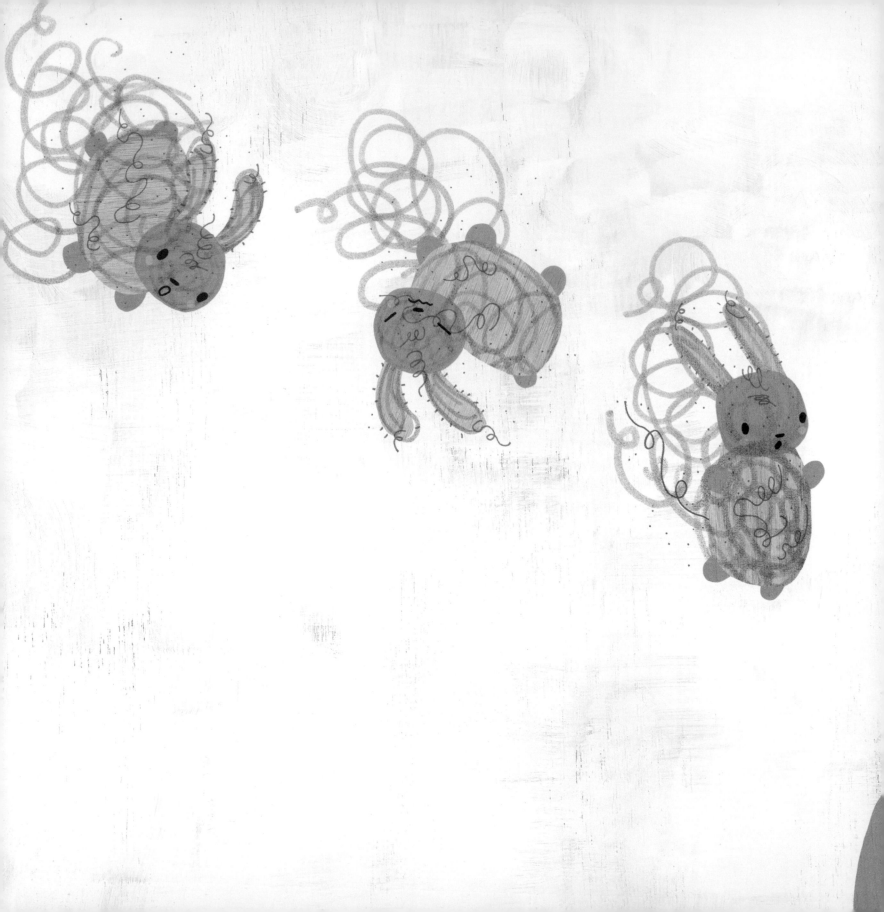

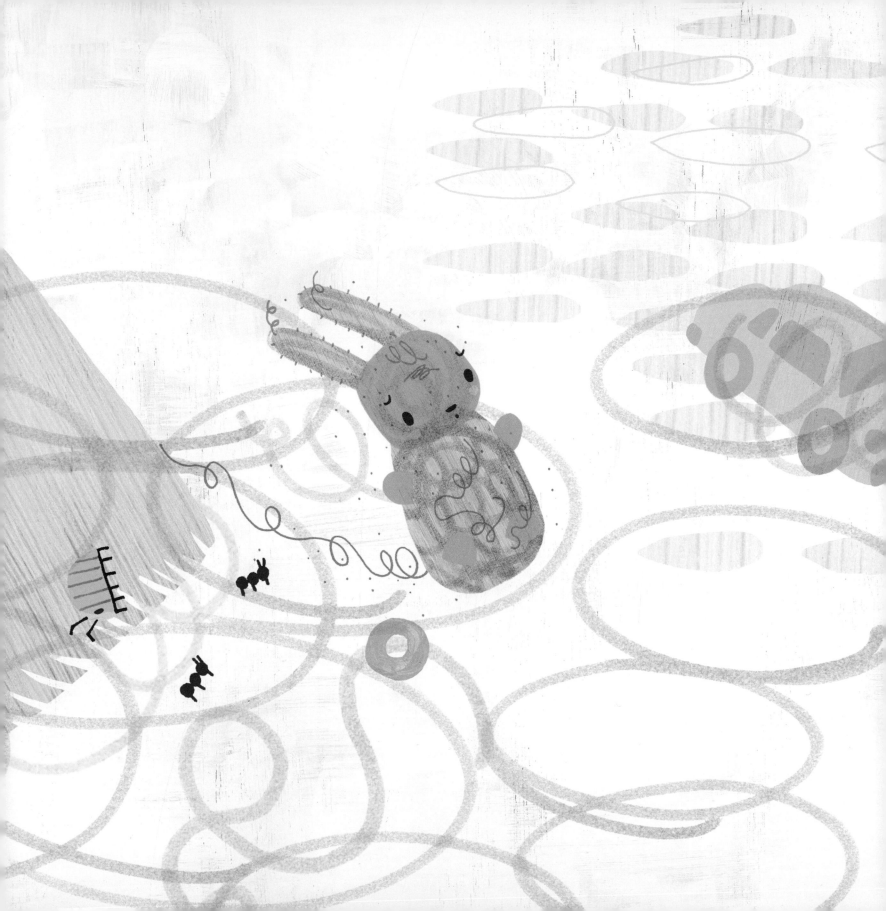

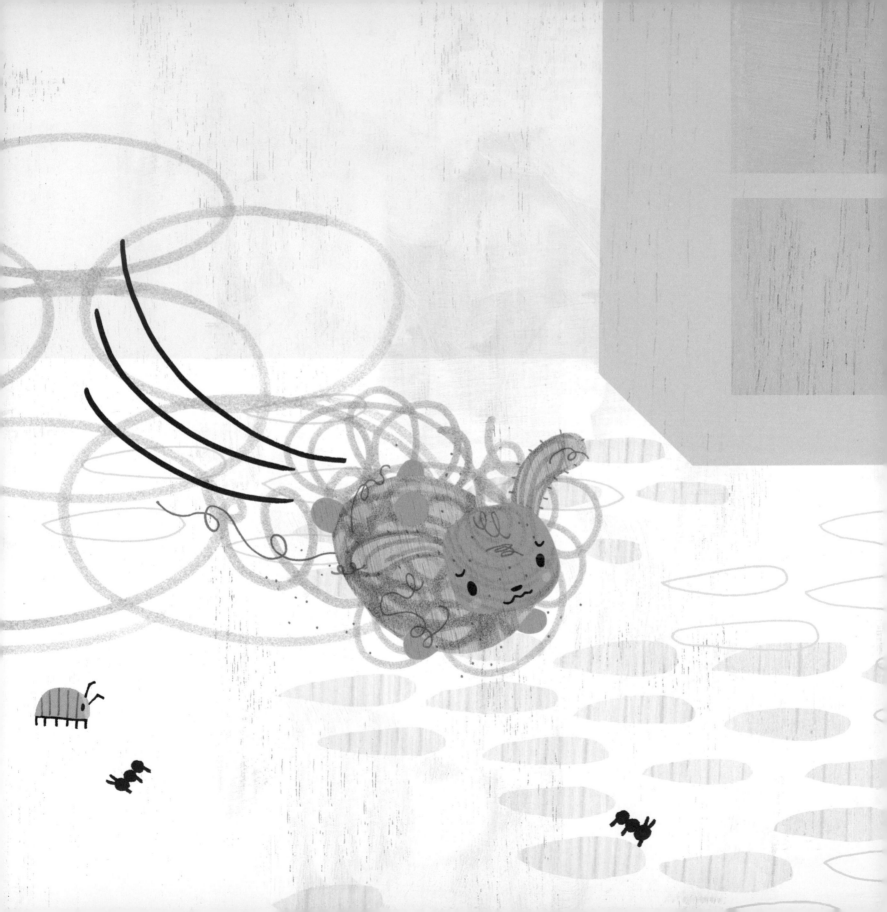

for scott — thank you for helping
to make this dream come true

Copyright © 2019 by Amy Hevron

All rights reserved. Published in the United States by Schwartz & Wade Books, an imprint of Random House Children's Books,
a division of Penguin Random House LLC, New York.

Schwartz & Wade Books and the colophon are trademarks of Penguin Random House LLC.

Visit us on the Web! rhcbooks.com

Educators and librarians, for a variety of teaching tools, visit us at RHTeachersLibrarians.com

Library of Congress Cataloging-in-Publication Data is available upon request.
ISBN 978-1-5247-6569-9 (hc)
ISBN 978-1-5247-6570-5 (lib. bdg.)
ISBN 978-1-5247-6571-2 (ebook)

The illustrations in this book were rendered in acrylic and marker on wood, collaged digitally.

MANUFACTURED IN CHINA
10 9 8 7 6 5 4 3 2 1
First Edition